STORYBOOK

Contents

TRANSFORMERS
RESCUE BOTS

Meet Chase
the Police-Bot

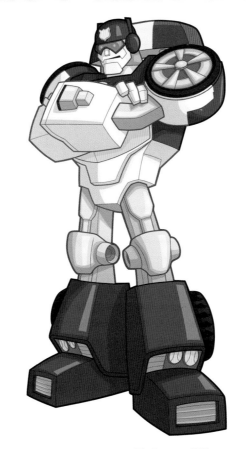

Adapted by **Lisa Shea**

Based on the episode
Family of Heroes written by
Nicole Dubuc

I am Chase the Police-Bot.
I am part of a special group
of Transformers called
the Rescue Bots.

Optimus Prime gave us a mission
to serve and protect humans.
The other Rescue Bots are named
Heatwave, Boulder and Blades.

I can turn into a police car.
My lights flash when I blast my siren.
I am fast on wheels!

I have a human partner.
His name is Chief Burns.
I enjoy working with the chief.
We do not let anyone break the law!

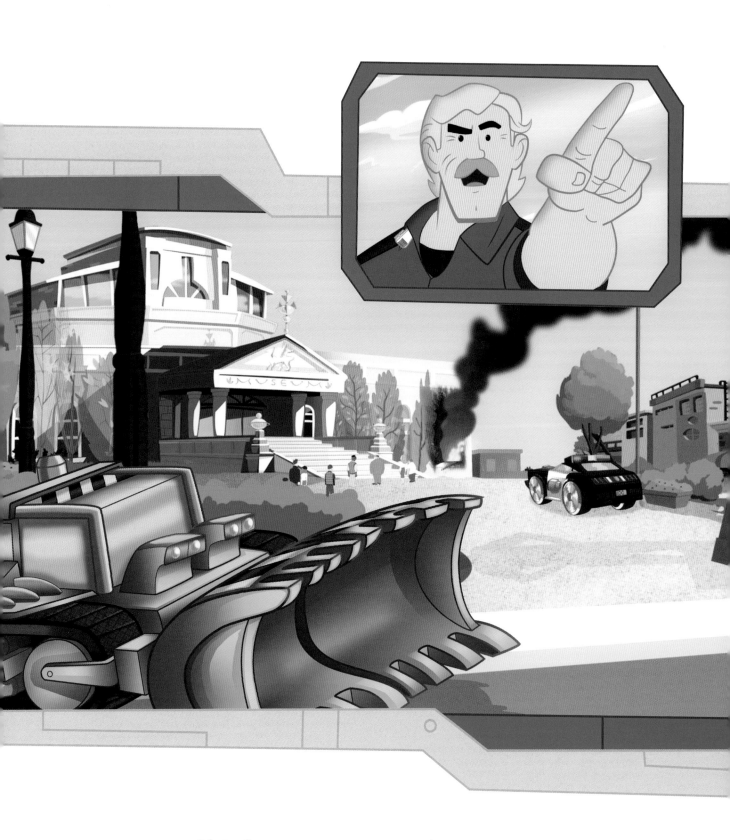

Chief Burns gets an alert.
The museum is on fire!
It is time for the other Rescue Bots
and I to go on our first mission!

Chief Burns asks me to make sure
all humans get out safely.
I do my job.
"Leave, please," I tell the humans.

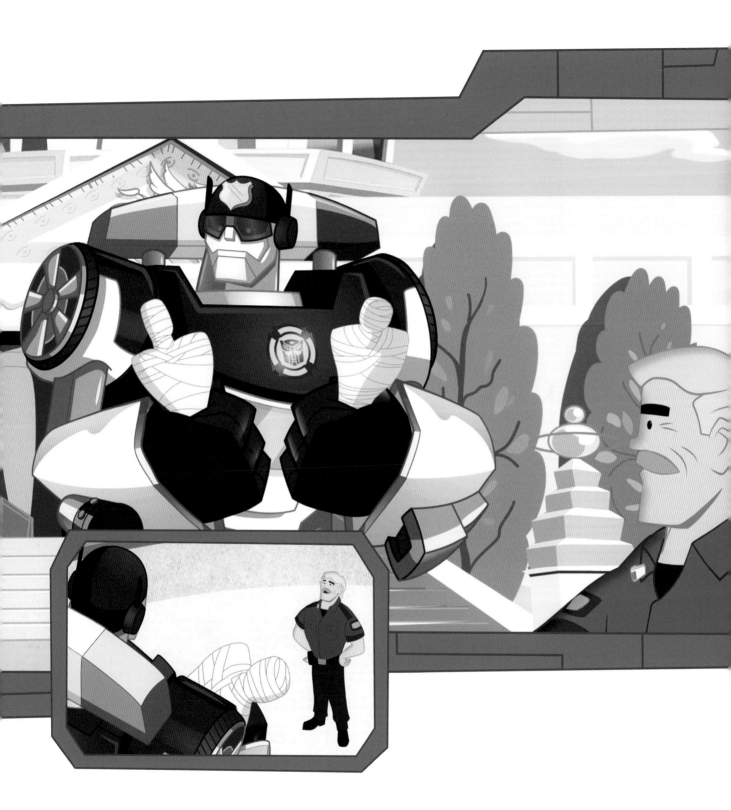

I am very polite, and I do not yell.
But two humans do not respond,
so I arrest them.
Chief Burns calls them mummies.

Inside the museum,
a dinosaur robot
is about to fall on a human!
The chief runs in to help.

Heatwave is team leader
of the Rescue Bots.
He acts fast to catch the robot
and save both humans!

The Rescue Bots pretend
to be regular robots.
We are really alien life forms.
Chief's family knows our secret.

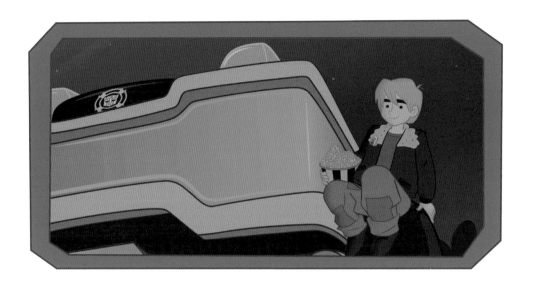

Chief Burns asks his son Cody
to help us hide in plain sight.
That night, Cody takes us to a movie
to learn about Earth.

Blades sees something and asks,
"Is that part of the show?"
There is a T. rex robot on the loose!

It came from the museum.
"The fire messed up the wires
inside the robot. Chase, turn
on your lights!" says Cody.

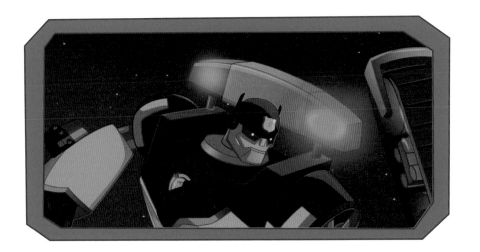

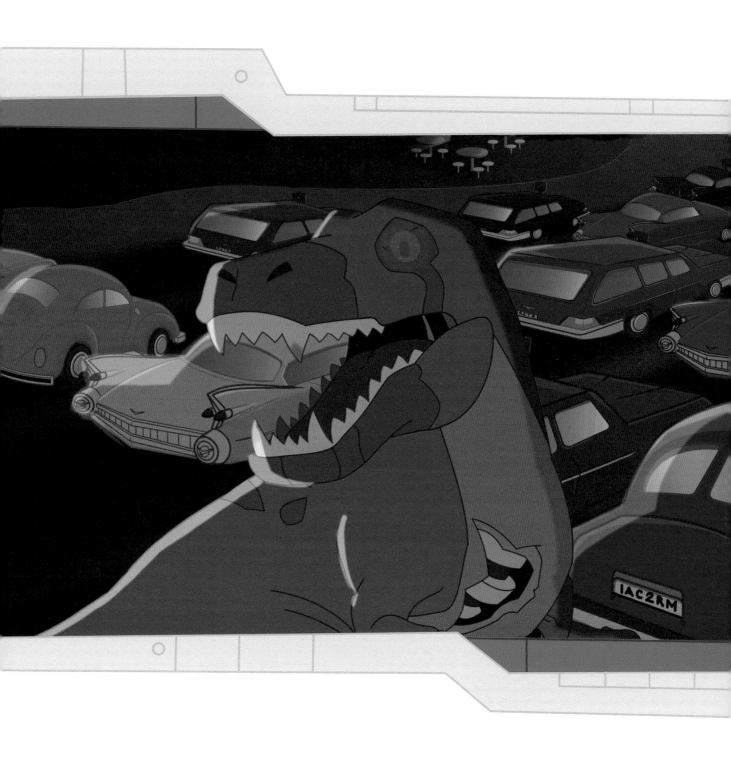

The T. rex turns around
and runs to me.
That is what we want.
We want it to leave the humans alone.

"Now what?" I ask.
To keep people safe,
we agree to lead the T. rex robot
to a place that has no humans.

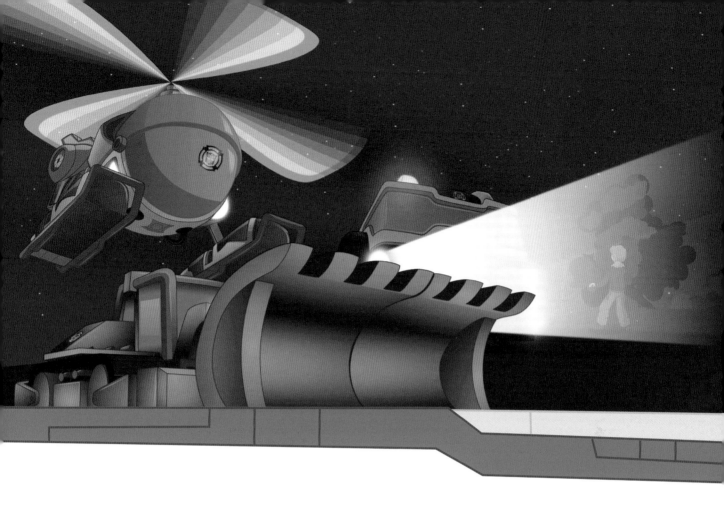

We change into our vehicles.
"Rescue Bots, roll to the rescue!"
says Heatwave.

Blades needs to get a cage.
To give him time to do that,
I race around with lights flashing.
That keeps the dino bot busy.

Next, we need the T. rex to sit down.
Heatwave knows what to do.
He waits for the right moment
and then slams the T. rex into the mud!

Blades is back!
He drops a metal cage on the T. rex.
Cody sneaks up and flips a switch.
He turns off the robot's power!

The chief is proud of Cody.
He puts him on the rescue team.
"I want a picture of all my heroes,"
he says as he takes a photo.

Wherever there is an emergency,
on land, in the sky or in the sea,
there are the Rescue Bots!

Even if the emergency is just keeping humans cool on a hot day!

The Rescue Bots are always ready
to roll to the rescue!

Meet
Heatwave
the Fire-Bot

Adapted by **Lisa Shea**

Based on the episode
Flobsters on Parade written by
Brian Hohlfeld

I am Heatwave.
I am the team leader of a special group
called the Rescue Bots.

Optimus Prime gave us a mission
to serve and protect humans.
My team members are
Chase, Boulder and Blades.

I change into a fire truck and work
with a human named Kade.
Kade knows my secret.

My secret is that I am an alien.
All the Rescue Bots are aliens.
We pretend to be Earth robots to fit in.

The town prepares for a parade.
Doc Greene fills a big balloon.
The balloon is shaped like a lobster.
Doc gets tangled up in a string and
floats away!

I know what to do.
My ladder goes up in the air.
Kade climbs up.
Together, we save Doc Greene!

Doc and his daughter Frankie
thank Kade but not me!
Doc thinks I am a normal robot
and I do not have feelings.
That makes me mad.
I am not just a robot.

The next day, our friend Cody
teaches us a game.
It is called Simon Says.
"Simon says, lift your arms,"
Cody calls out.
We lift our arms.

"Lift your left leg," Cody says.
Blades and Boulder lift their legs.
"He did not say 'Simon says',"
Chase tells them.
"That is right, Chase," says Cody.
"Remember to do only what your
humans tell you to do."
Then we will seem like Earth robots.

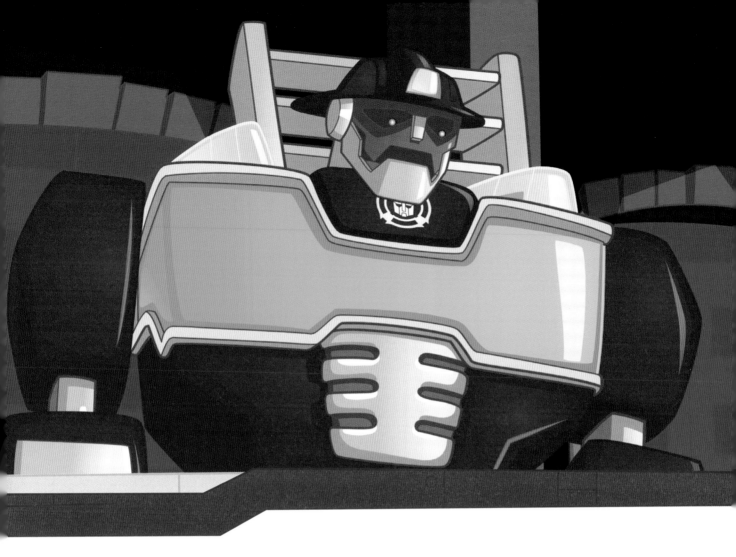

The Rescue Bots are going
to march in the parade.
We will pretend to be Earth robots.
I do not want to pretend.
"I will stay home," I say.

Chief Burns arrives to take
the Rescue Bots to the parade.
I pretend I am broken.
The group leaves without me.

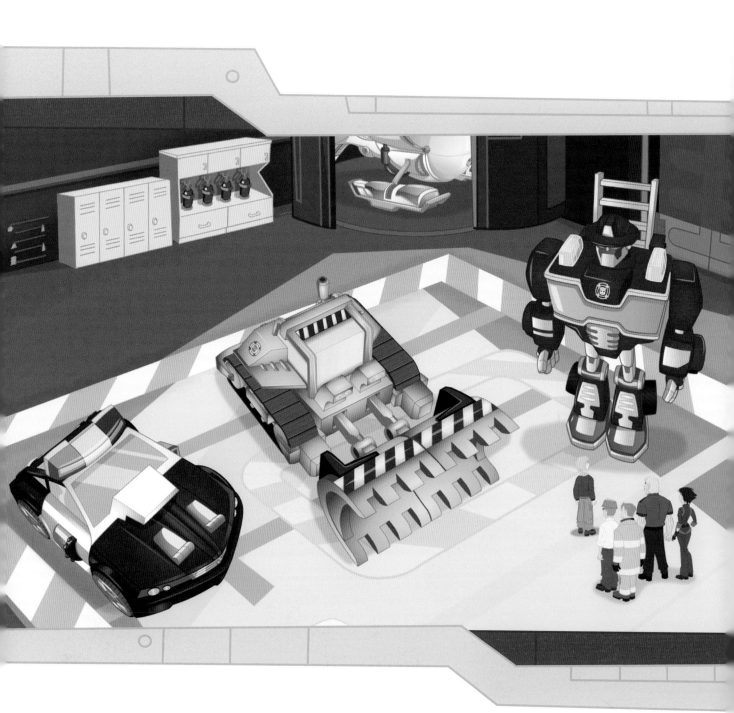

During the parade,
Doc Greene shows off a gas
he calls floatium.
Doc invented it to keep balloons
from floating away.

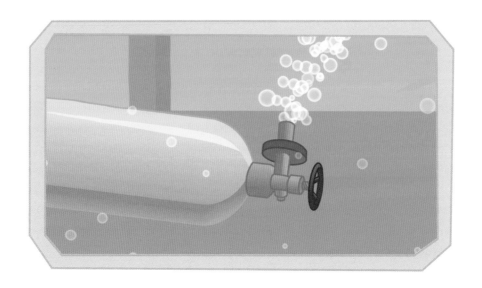

The floatium gas gets
into the lobster tank.
The lobsters start floating
in the air!

Cody and Frankie think the floating lobsters are funny. They call them flobsters!

"Oh, dear," says Doc Greene.
"The floatium will not wear off
for two more days!"
People try to jump and catch the flobsters.

I am at home.
Kade calls me,
but I do not answer.
I am still feeling sorry for myself.

I turn on the television.
I see floating lobsters!
The flobsters attack the mayor
while he makes a speech!

The other Rescue Bots do the best
they can to protect the humans.
I can see on TV that they still need help.

Lobsters like to eat starfish!
The flobsters think the starfish
on Frankie's jacket is real.
She hides in a phone booth.

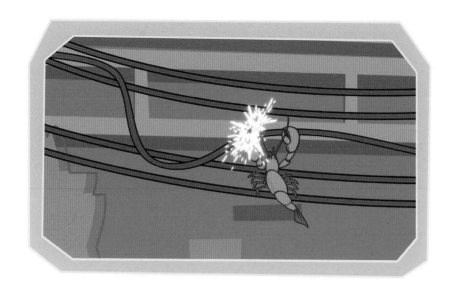

The flobsters attack!
I need to stop feeling mad.
My team needs me.
Kade needs me.

I rush into town to join the fight.
My fire hoses spray the flobsters
with massive water power.

The flobsters are afraid of the giant
lobster balloon. We herd them into
a trap using the balloon.
I spray them back into the tank!

We saved the parade!
Everyone says the Rescue Bots
are heroes. I feel so happy.

Meet
Blades
the Copter-Bot

Adapted by **D. Jakobs**

Based on the episode
Under Pressure written by
Nicole Dubuc

Earth is very strange to the Rescue Bots.

Blades is having a hard time in
his new home.

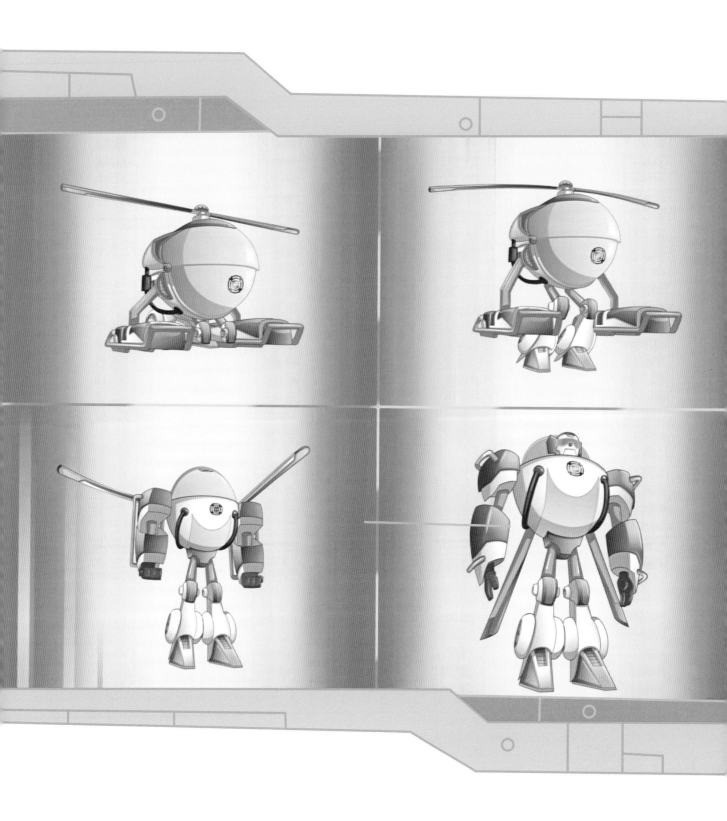

On Cybertron, Blades was a land vehicle.
He had wheels!
But here on Earth,
he changes into a helicopter.

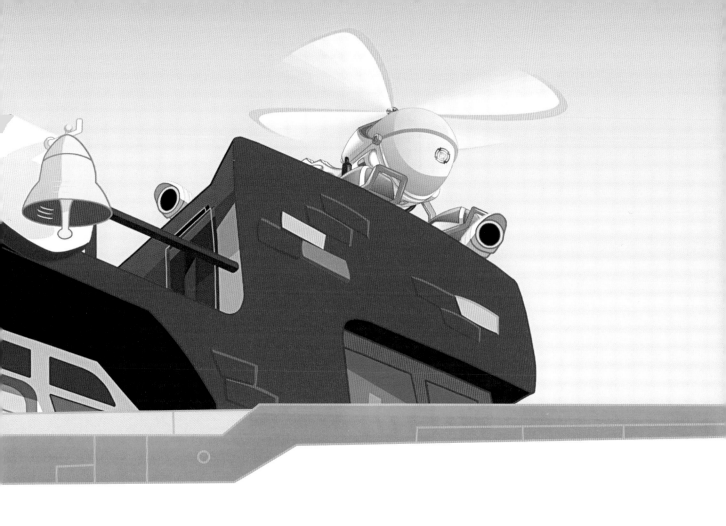

Helicopters do not ride on the ground.
They fly!
Blades is scared of heights!

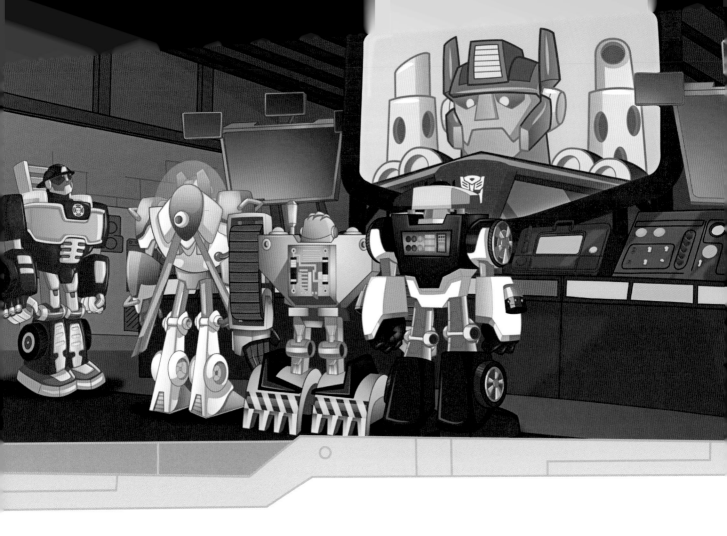

Blades has to be brave and fly
so he can do what Optimus Prime told him.
Blades's human partner, Dani, loves to fly.

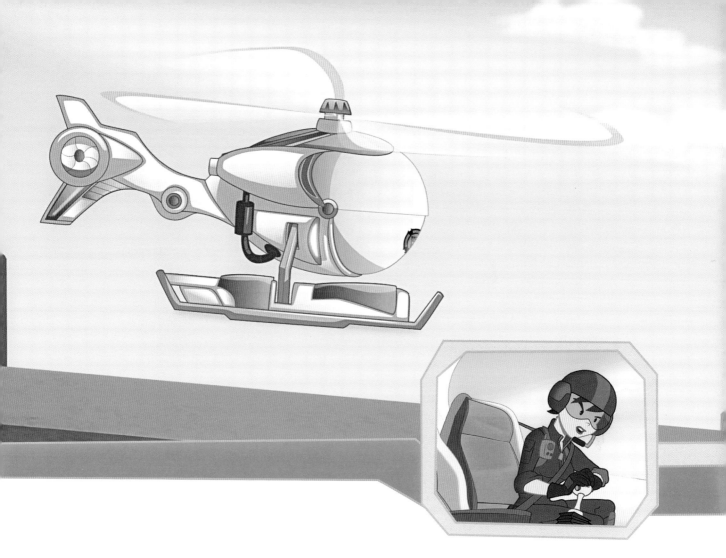

When they are flying together, she pulls hard at his controls and yells at him. "Hurry up, Blades!" she says. "Go higher!"

Cody gets his family and the Rescue Bots
together in the bunker.
He wants them to like and respect one another.

Blades and Dani try to be friends.

"Er, do you have any hobbies?" asks Blades.

"Flying," says Dani.

Blades does not like this answer.

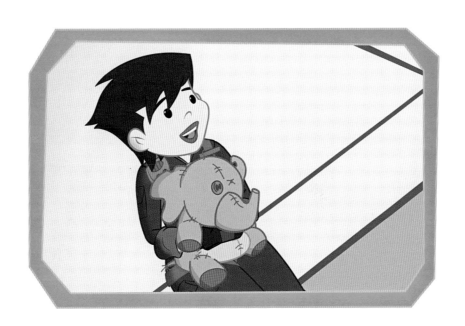

Just then, the town's fake volcano
starts erupting real lava!
Lava is rock that is so hot, it flows.
It can burn anything in its path.
The team leaps into action.

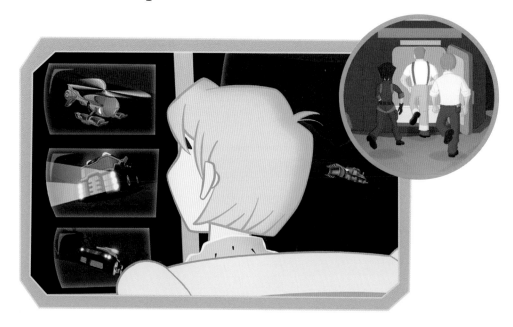

Blades and Dani need to fly into the crater and flip a switch before the volcano explodes.

"Ow! Can you be more gentle?" asks Blades.
"As soon as you learn to fly," says Dani.

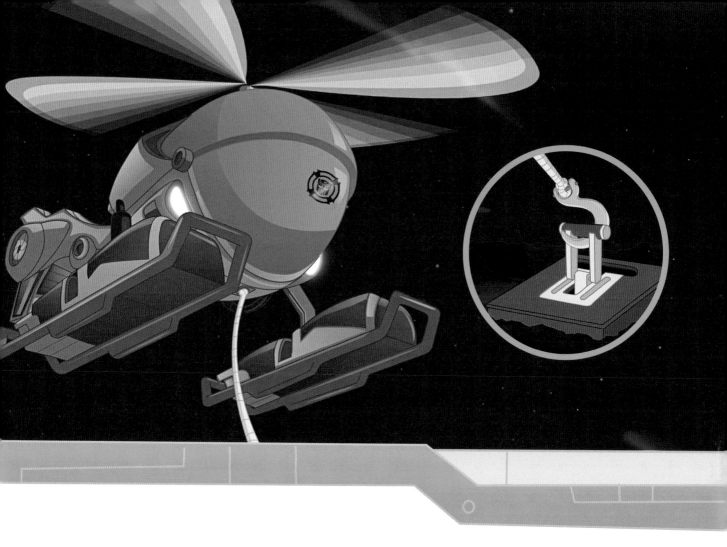

They need to fly fast and high.
The flying is scarier to Blades
than the lava, but he flips the switch!

"We did it!" says Dani.

BOOM!

A cloud of ash bursts from the volcano.

Blades cannot see a thing!

"Fly higher!" yells Dani.

"Which way is higher?" says Blades.

"Talk nicely to Blades, Dani,"
says Cody from the command centre.

Dani and Blades work together
to get away from the ash and lava.
They are happy,
but the emergency is not over.

The leftover lava is heading
down the tunnels towards Cody!

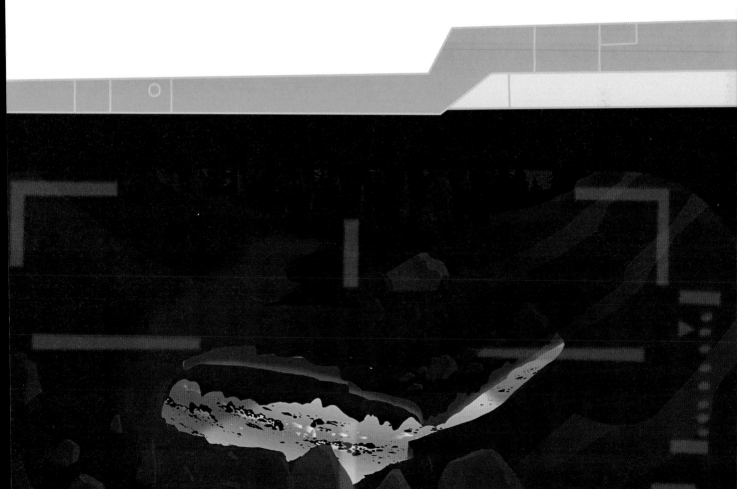

They need to cool the lava
and turn it back into rock quickly!

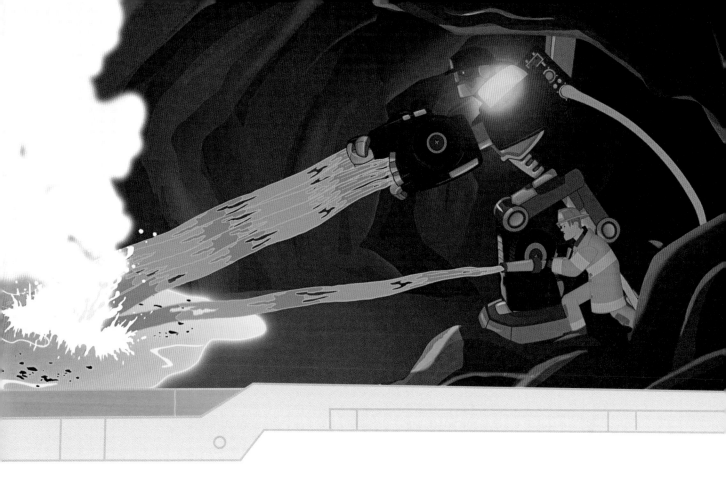

Heatwave and Kade try to
stop the lava, but the tanks
run out of water.

There is a huge water tower nearby,
but the ash cloud is in the way.
Only Blades can get there in time.

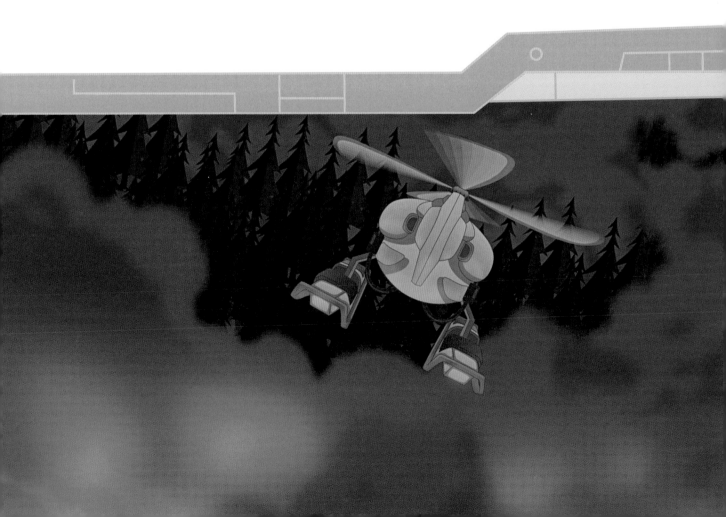

"The ash may hurt your rotors," says Dani.
"It is worth it to help Cody!" says Blades.

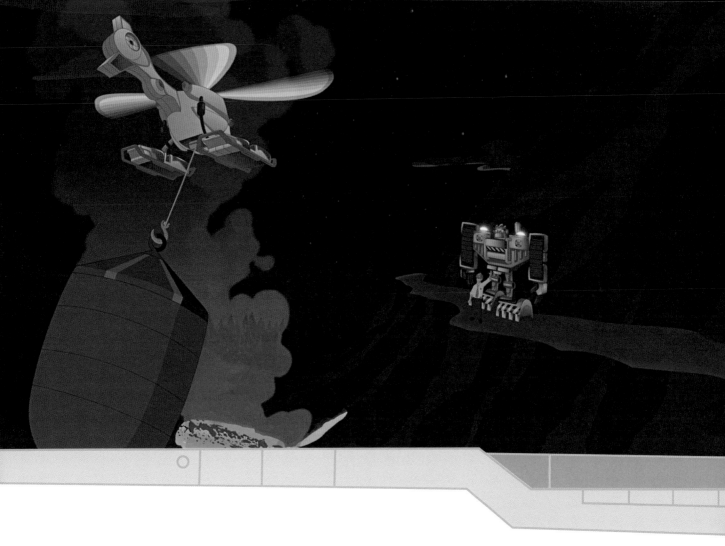

With Dani's help, Blades soars through the smoke and picks up the water tower. Together, they save the day.

"We did it, partner!" says Dani.
They both feel very proud.

Blades finally feels at home.

Meet
Boulder
the Construction-Bot

Adapted by Annie Auerbach

Based on the episode
Walk on the Wild Side written by
Nicole Dubuc

The phone rings in the firehouse.
"Emergency! Come right away!"
the chief hears the caller say.

"It could be a fire!" says Dani.
"Or a broken pipe!" says Graham.
The Rescue Bots change form.
The humans jump inside and go.

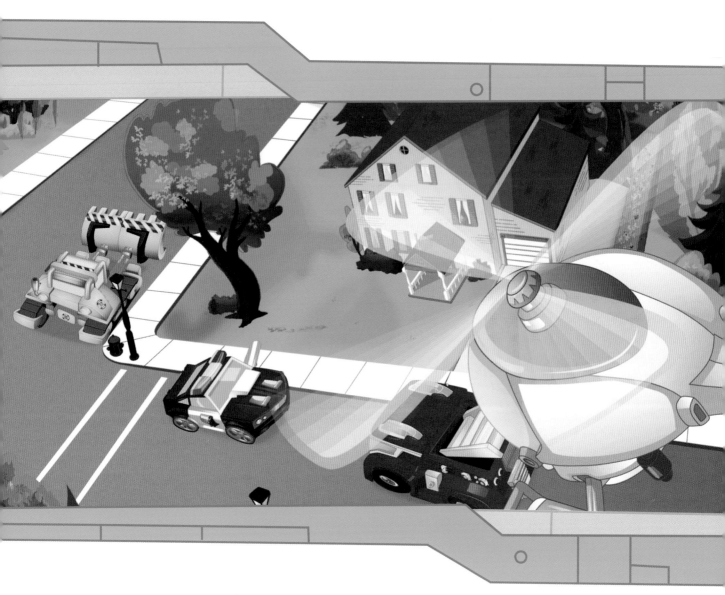

They arrive at a house.
What a surprise!
It is just a cat stuck in a tree!

Boulder changes back into a robot.
He helps the cat climb onto his body.
The owner is happy.

Later, Boulder asks Cody about pets.
Cody thinks pets are very cool.
"Some pets even work on rescue teams,"
Cody says.
"Wow!" says Boulder.

Now Boulder wants to get a pet
for the rescue team.
He wants it to be a surprise.
So Blades and Boulder sneak out at night.

Boulder wants to find a pet
at the zoo!

The gates are locked.
Boulder turns off the power.
The gates unlock and all the
cages open.

"Here is the perfect pet!"
He points to a large lion.
It reminds him of the cat that he rescued.
"We can call it Whiskers," says Boulder.

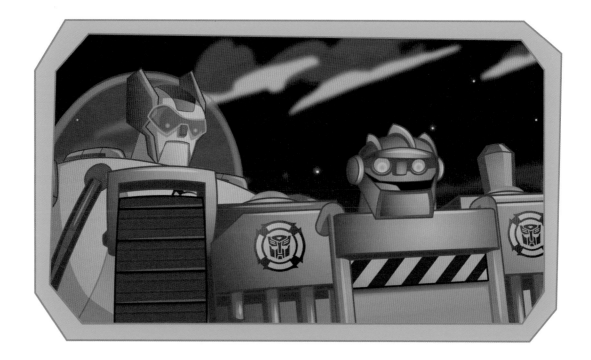

The lion roars.
It leaps out of its cage
and into a tree.

Then it jumps over the zoo wall.
The lion has escaped!

The next day, Chief Burns gets
a call for help.
He and the rescue team rush
out to find the lion in a tree!

"We found my pet!"
says Boulder.

"That is no pet," Graham says.
"That is a wild animal.
It needs to go back to the zoo!"
"Human ways are so confusing,"
says Boulder.

The lion jumps from the tree.
Chase tries to grab it but misses.
The team must catch the lion!
"Rescue Bots, roll to the rescue!"
says Heatwave.

Boulder drives up on one side of the lion.
Heatwave drives up on the other side.
The lion snarls and growls. It is trapped.

"Now!" shouts Graham.
Blades drops down a huge crate.

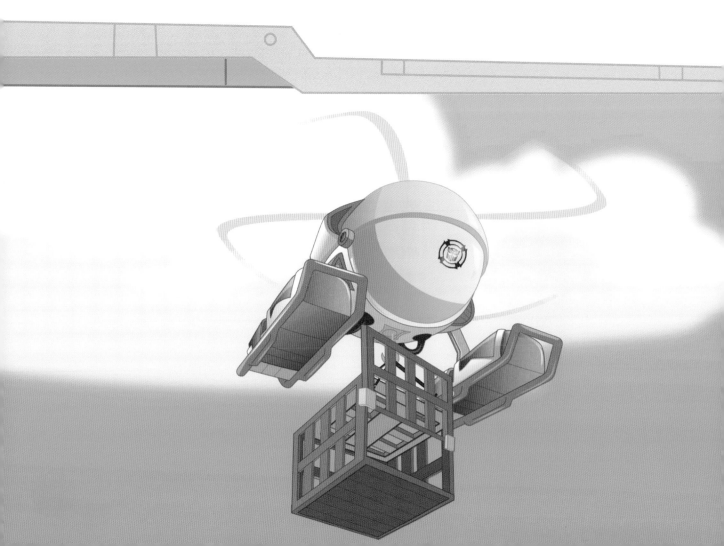

The lion is locked in the crate!
"Great catch!" says Cody.

The animal is put back in the zoo.
The mayor makes sure the cage is locked.

"Whiskers was too much work,"
Boulder tells the team.
"But it would be nice to have a pet."

"I know how you feel," says Cody.
"So I got you something to care for."

Cody hands Boulder a plant.
"Come on, boy," Boulder says to the plant.
"Want to play catch?"

Cody laughs and shakes his head.
"Boulder!" he says.
"Plants do not play catch!"

TRANSFORMERS RESCUE BOTS

The Mystery of the Pirate Bell

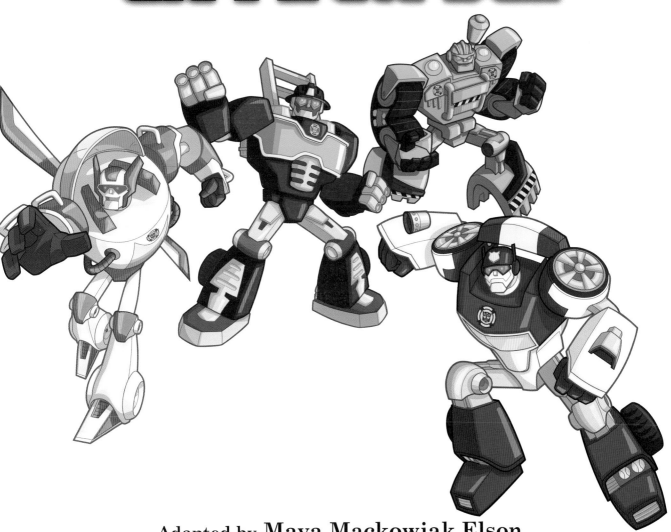

Adapted by Maya Mackowiak Elson

Based on the episode
The Lost Bell written by
Greg Johnson

Cody is telling the Rescue Bots about an important event in Griffin Rock history. "Pirates sailed in on a ship called the *Oaken Crow*, and looted!" he says.

"Of all the things they stole, the Settlers' Bell was the most valuable. It had hung in the lighthouse tower since the town's founding," Cody explains. "What happened to the pirates?" Blades asks.

Just as Cody is about to tell them, his dad, Chief Burns, stops him with some news. "A storm is about to make landfall, and we need to button down the town," he says.

Chief Burns signals to the Rescue Bots to prepare for the bad weather.
They pick up branches from the street, board up windows, and secure traffic-bots.

"So, what did happen to the pirates?" Blades asks.
"They sailed into a storm like this one," Cody says.
"The *Oaken Crow* disappeared, and nobody ever
heard from them again!"

Rain begins to fall hard as the team is securing equipment at the marina. A bolt of lightning knocks over a huge shipping container, breaking the pier. Cody and the Rescue Bots are washed out to sea!

The storm is too strong for any human
to follow after them.
Soon, Cody and the Rescue Bots find
themselves in calmer waters, and they
go ashore on a deserted beach.

"We're castaways!" Cody exclaims.
"Isn't that cool?"
"You know what would be cooler?"
Blades sighs. "If my rotor wasn't
bent. Then I could fly for help!"

Cody and the Rescue Bots discover a small clearing with a waterfall and a stream.

"This is a good place for a shelter," Cody says.

"One shelter, coming up!" Heatwave exclaims.

The Rescue Bots start building an unsteady
structure of rocks, mud, and logs. As Boulder
opens the door, the shelter collapses into a pile.
"It's okay, guys," Cody says when he sees the
ruins. "I built my own."

Cody's shelter is small, simple, and just right.
"How did you learn to build that?" Heatwave asks.
"Lad Pioneers," Cody says. "See? It pays to learn
about history and how things were done in the
past."

With a shelter built, Cody realizes he's very
hungry. The Rescue Bots are determined
to find their friend some food.
They search the beach and tide pool but
find very little.

The Rescue Bots return to Cody without any food. Luckily, Cody has found some fish from the stream! "Don't worry. You tried," says Cody. "Do you know what I really need? Firewood!"

The Rescue Bots gather lots of wood and use it to make an enormous fire.

"Let's tell spooky stories," Cody says. "I know a good one. Five friends are in a dark and creepy forest..."

This is enough to scare Blades.
"The fire needs more fuel!" he says as he
jumps up and leaves the fire. He returns with
a large chunk of wood.
"Something is carved into that," Cody
exclaims. "It's a crow! Like the figurehead on
the pirate ship!"

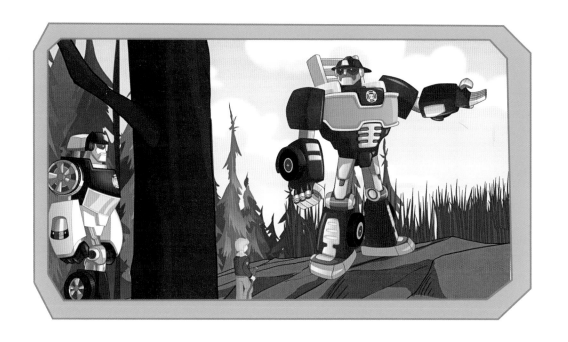

The next morning, Cody and the Rescue Bots go to the ridge where Blades found the crow figurehead. Suddenly, they fall to the bottom of a dimly lit cavern!

"You will never believe what we just found!" Cody says as he leads the Rescue Bots around a bend. The *Oaken Crow* is floating in a large grotto!
"It looks like it came through there," Boulder says, pointing to an opening blocked by rocks.

"Let's see what's on board!" Cody exclaims.
He sprints up the gangplank and leaps on
board. There, on the deck of the ship, is the
long-lost Settlers' Bell!

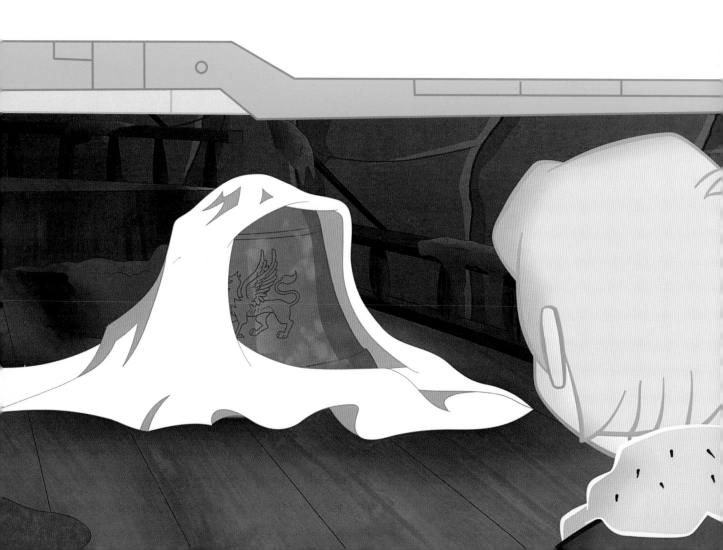

"What a work of art," says Boulder.
"I can't believe the Settlers' Bell can
finally return home!" Cody says.

Cody realizes that the ship has been stuck down there for centuries. How will they get it out?

"This calls for the help of a state-of-the-art Rescue Bot," says Chase.

The Rescue Bots get to work clearing
rocks and securing rigging. Soon they
emerge from the cavern with the ship.

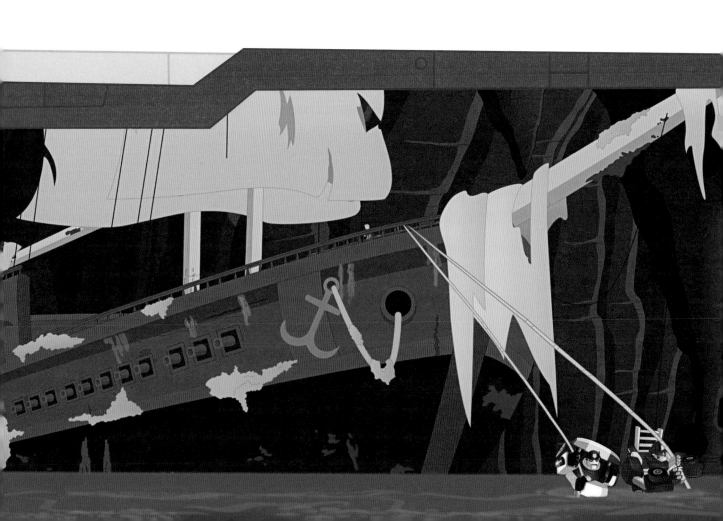

Back at Griffin Rock, the Settlers' Bell is in the lighthouse tower again. The town gathers for this historic occasion, and Cody and his fellow Lad Pioneers have the special privilege of ringing the bell in celebration!

"This will require a new chapter to be written in the Griffin Rock history book," Chase says. Boulder smiles. "Maybe we'll be mentioned."

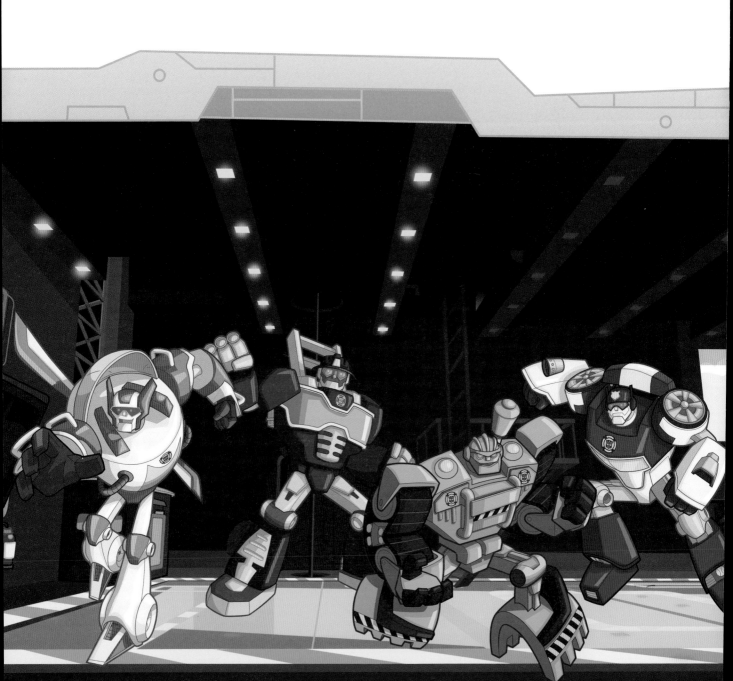